GOOD D🐾G 6

Life Is Good

by
Cam Higgins

illustrated by
Ariel Landy

LITTLE SIMON

New York   London   Toronto   Sydney   New Delhi

LITTLE SIMON
An imprint of Simon & Schuster Children's Publishing Division
1230 Avenue of the Americas, New York, New York 10020
First Little Simon paperback edition October 2021
Copyright © 2021 by Simon & Schuster, Inc.
Also available in a Little Simon hardcover edition

For information about special discounts for bulk purchases, please contact Simon & Schuster Special Sales at 1-866-506-1949 or business@simonandschuster.com.
The Simon & Schuster Speakers Bureau can bring authors to your live event. For more information or to book an event contact the Simon & Schuster Speakers Bureau at 1-866-248-3049 or visit our website at www.simonspeakers.com.
Designed by Leslie Mechanic
Manufactured in the United States of America 1023 LAK
10 9 8 7 6 5
Library of Congress Cataloging-in-Publication Data
Names: Higgins, Cam, author. | Landy, Ariel, illustrator.
Title: Life is good / by Cam Higgins; illustrated by Ariel Landy.
Description: First Little Simon edition. | New York: Little Simon, 2021. | Series: Good dog; 6 | Audience: Ages 5–9.
Summary: Farm puppy Bo experiences snow for the first time.
Identifiers: LCCN 2021006102 (print) | LCCN 2021006103 (ebook) | ISBN 9781534495371 (paperback) | ISBN 9781534495388 (hardcover) | ISBN 9781534495395 (ebook)
Subjects: CYAC: Dogs—Fiction. | Animals—Infancy—Fiction. | Snow—Fiction. | Domestic animals—Fiction. | Farm life—Fiction.
Classification: LCC PZ7.1.H54497 Li 2021 (print) | LCC PZ7.1.H54497 (ebook) | DDC [Fic]—dc23
LC record available at https://lccn.loc.gov/2021006102

CONTENTS

A
Cold Snap

There was something in the air. Something new, with a sharp, tangy smell. All of us could sense it.

The chicks were waddling a little faster. The sheep grew a bit fluffier. The pigs—well, they always eat . . . but for some reason, they started eating a lot more.

It all started one chilly morning when a wisp of white cloud blew right out of my mouth. I was outside with Wyatt and Imani, my human brother and sister, while they were doing their daily chores on the farm.

I stopped in my tracks as soon as I saw the first white puff. I was so surprised! It looked super yummy, so I opened my mouth wide. But it disappeared before I could bite it.

"Bo!" Imani laughed as she watched me chase the white puffs. "Silly dog, that's your own breath. When it's cold out, you can see your breath when you breathe out. Here, watch."

Imani blew out a big white cloud that floated in the air. She looked like a fire-breathing dragon from one of those books she liked to read. Hmm, did this mean Imani could breathe real fire too? I hoped not!

"Looks like we're in for a cold snap," said Wyatt. "Maybe it will even snow!"

Imani jumped toward the sky and cheered. "Oooh, I sure hope so!"

Every once in a while, humans use a word I've never heard before. Like "spoon." I learned that word last week when I got caught licking a *spoon* in the dishwasher. I was just copying what I saw them doing all the time, but Imani told me I was *not* allowed to lick spoons.

I also learned the word "socks" when I was a young pup. And here's a secret: dirty socks might *smell* bad, but they taste amazing! Like spoons, I'm not supposed to eat them, either. But of course I still like to try!

And now I had a new word to learn: "snow."

2

A Good
Fancy Word

Snow, snow, snow . . . I said the word over and over again in my head. Was it a big thing? Was it small? Was it yummy? I really hoped it was yummy. Yummy things are the best!

As I wondered about this new fancy word, Wyatt and Imani went on their way about the farm.

I watched as they poured a mix of food scraps and grains into the trough for the pigs. My buddy Zonks was there, and I thought he might know about snow. I followed Imani and Wyatt over to his pen.

"Hey, Zonks," I said. "Wyatt said it might snow!"

Zonks had perked up as soon as Imani and Wyatt walked over. "That's cool," Zonks said between bites. Then he said something else, too, but his mouth was full, so it came out really muffled. Pigs can be like that. A good breakfast is very important to them.

So I decided to follow Wyatt and Imani to the barn to help feed the horses. I took the chance to talk to my friend Comet the foal.

"Hey, Comet, guess what? Wyatt said there might be snow on the way," I told her.

She kicked up her hooves in excitement. "Snow? Really? I can't believe it. That sounds wonderful! But . . . Bo, I have a question: What is snow?" she asked.

"I don't know yet, but I do know that it's a *good* fancy word!" I replied, shrugging.

She blinked at me a few times and then said, "Uh-huh. Well, whatever snow is, I can't wait!"

As she turned back to munch on her hay, I wandered farther into the barn . . . and guess who I ran into? The barn cats, King and Diva.

King and Diva aren't exactly the nicest animals on the farm. In fact, they like to tease puppies like me. But luckily, today they didn't seem interested in me at all. They just stared out the window longingly. And I couldn't help but wonder if they were waiting for snow too.

Where Are You, Snow?

No one knew when the snow was coming. What if we had to wait a really long time? Well, if that was the case, there was only one thing to do: go searching for snow myself!

I crept around the farm, trying to stay hidden. I sure didn't want to scare the snow away!

So I hid behind some bushes by the front gate. The front gate is where humans enter when they come to the farm—like the delivery-truck driver who comes with packages.

Wait! That's it! Maybe someone was going to *deliver* snow!

When the mail truck came, I watched it like a hawk. Mr. Jones, the mail carrier, stepped out and waved to me.

"Hiya, Bo! It looks like you're waiting for something important," he said. "But I only have a few letters today. Sorry!"

I gave Mr. Jones a friendly woof, then sat back and watched a few more trucks drive by. But no one stopped at our house. It didn't seem like anyone was going to deliver snow. So it was time to continue my search.

You can find so many different things in the forest—like pine cones and bunnies and squirrels (who always need chasing). I hid behind a tree and tucked myself low to the ground.

As I waited, I realized it was extra quiet in the woods. Maybe the forest animals were all waiting for snow too!

That's when something floated down from the sky. I watched as it drifted along, twirling lightly in the air. As soon as it hit the ground, I pounced, trapping it between my paws.

Carefully, I lifted my paw to take a peek. Only it wasn't snow. It was just a normal leaf. It must have fallen from the tree that I was sitting under. Turns out, my search wasn't over.

So I kept going until I spotted something shiny on the ground. It caught the sunlight shining down through the trees and reflected its glow. What could it be? I rushed over to check it out.

But I zoomed and slid right over it! This wasn't snow. It was a frozen puddle!

When I got back on my paws, I leaned over to study it. I looked down and saw my reflection. But that wasn't all I saw. There were pieces of white fluff floating all around me! What could this be?

I looked up and realized that the white flakes weren't just falling onto the frozen puddle. *How will I ever find snow with all this white stuff getting in the way everywhere?* I wondered.

Then one of the flakes landed on my nose. It was cold and a little bit wet. But it was also soft and absolutely magical! I tried to lick it, but it disappeared way too fast.

I looked down at the ground as the flakes started to stick to the grass.

As I watched a fluffy white blanket cover the ground, that's when it hit me. *This* must be snow.

Snow Paws

I raced back to the farm. The snow was falling everywhere! It was piling up on the branches of the trees. It was on the barn roof. The grass was almost completely covered.

The entire world was turning white right before my puppy eyes! And I didn't want my friends to miss it.

So I ran to Zonks first. He was
squealing with joy and hopping
around his pen. "You see, Bo! I told
you snow was magical!"

"Is that what you said to me
this morning?" I asked. "I couldn't
understand you because your mouth
was full of food."

"Oh, I guess you need to learn how to speak pig. It's a mouthful," Zonks said with a happy snort. "But what are you waiting for? Come on in! Let's play in the snow!"

First we played tag. As I ran across
the pen, the cold snow felt nice and
soft on my paws. Then we played roll-
around-in-the-snow. It was lots of fun,
but we didn't get dirty like we usually
do when we're in mud.

After a little while Comet and her parents strolled by.

"Hey, Comet, do you want to play?" I asked.

"I'm sorry, Bo, but horses aren't allowed in the pigpen," Comet told me.

"Oh, okay, but I hope you enjoy the snow too," I replied.

Next a few of the chicks scooted by the pigpen, so I asked them if they wanted to play. The snow was starting to really pile up, so their tiny orange legs were almost completely buried!

"Sorry, Bo, we can't play today," they chirped. "We need to get home to the nest, where it's warm and snug."

I nodded my head as they moved along. I didn't mind because that meant Zonks and I could keep running around together. We rolled in the snow some more, but soon my puppy legs got cold, cold, COLD!

"Zonks, aren't you freezing?" I asked my friend.

"Nope, not at all," he said as he pointed to his big belly. "I've been eating extra to prepare for the winter, so the cold doesn't bother me."

"What? Oh, no, I haven't prepared anything!" I whimpered. I was totally soaked and shivering, which meant it was time to go home.

5

Warm and Cozy

As I stepped back inside the house, a rush of heat swept over me. It felt so doggone good! My puppy paws started to tingle, and that's when it hit me. I had been playing outside in the freezing cold!

I headed straight for the fireplace and let my body warm up.

But soon I started to feel lonely.
After playing with my friends, I missed
having company.

My human family was all snuggled together on the couch, talking in quiet voices and watching the snow fall outside the window. That couch was exactly where I wanted to be!

I stuck my nose in between Jennica and Darnell, my human mom and dad.

"No, Bo," Jennica said gently. "There's no room here."

I moved to where Imani and Wyatt were perched and tried to hop up onto the cushion between them.

"Silly Bo! You can't fit!" Imani laughed, scratching my head.

"All right, everyone. I think it's time for a snow-day treat. How about some hot chocolate?" Darnell said, getting up from the couch.

I looked at the space he had left open on the sofa, then watched as he headed for the kitchen. I love watching humans cook. The smells are delicious, and if I'm lucky, I get the scraps that fall on the floor! I followed Darnell into the kitchen.

First he melted some chocolate chips in a pan, and then he added milk and stirred everything together as it warmed over the stove. When it was ready, Darnell poured the hot chocolate into mugs, added marshmallows, and plopped a swirl of whipped cream on top that came squirting out of a can with a loud *WHOOSH*!

The sound made me jump, so I barked right back. The can had better not try anything funny!

I watched as Darnell put the mugs onto a tray and brought the hot chocolate over to the family.

He passed out each mug and then placed a plate in front of me, too.

"You can't have hot chocolate, Bo," Darnell said. "It'll hurt your tummy. But you should still have your own little snow-day treat."

The plate was filled with whipped cream! It looked a little like snow, but it smelled much yummier. I took a deep sniff and felt something funny on the end of my nose.

It was cold and wet, but it didn't melt away like snow. I licked it off and couldn't believe it. It was the most delicious thing I'd ever tasted in my entire puppy life!

I finished my whipped cream in no time flat, and then I looked at the others, who were barely sipping their mugs. *Why do humans drink so slow? I thought.*

With my snow-day treat finished, I curled up on my favorite blanket near the fire and shut my eyes. I told myself it would be a quick nap. But I ended up sleeping through the night because it was just so cozy.

6

A Winter Wonderland

The next morning the sun's rays felt extra bright as I woke up from my spot in the den. I looked out the window and let out a yip of surprise.

The entire farm was covered in white, fluffy snow! Overnight, everything had changed.

After my humans and I ate
breakfast, I watched as Imani and
Wyatt put on many, many layers of
clothes.

It was hard to wait patiently, but
finally the three of us stepped out
the door . . . and straight into a
winter wonderland!

I barked happily as my paws sank into the snow with a small crunch. The fields were a blanket of sparkling white, and the branches on the trees were covered in snow. Since it was such an exciting day, Darnell offered to do Imani's and Wyatt's chores so that they could play with me outside.

"Hey, Bo!" Wyatt called out. Suddenly a white ball flashed through the air. "Fetch!"

I gave a bark and chased the snowball. But it had landed on the ground and vanished. I turned in circles trying to find it.

"Here's another one, Bo!" Imani shouted with a laugh.

I chased the next snowball as it arced through the air. I buried my face in the snow looking for it. I didn't find the ball, but I did come up with a mouthful of icy yumminess.

"Hey, I know—let's build a snowman!" Wyatt suggested. He shaped another snowball in his hands, packing it tight. I watched as he placed it on the ground and began to roll it across the lawn. The ball grew bigger and bigger, and I knew exactly what to do.

When Imani set another snowball on the ground, I ran over and pushed it forward. The cold wetness tickled my nose and made me sneeze. White powder flew up everywhere! Imani scratched behind my ears.

"Oh, Bo, you're such a funny pup," she said.

I watched as they piled three big snowballs on top of one another. Then Wyatt picked up a branch that was poking out of the snow and stuck it right in the middle of the snowman, giving it an arm.

"Hey, Bo, can you find another stick?"

Oh, you bet I could! Wyatt knew I was an expert at finding sticks! I ran to the big tree and sniffed around until I found the perfect stick, and then I raced back to Wyatt and Imani.

"Good boy, Bo!" Wyatt told me. Then he stuck it into the other side of the snowman.

After that, Imani placed a hat and scarf around it too, and she pushed rocks into the middle of its body and stood back. "Our snowman is now complete!" she cried.

I wagged my tail in excitement.
Today's fancy word was "snowman."

"Awesome! Now let's go sledding!"
Wyatt whooped. He grabbed the sled
from the porch, and we headed for
the big hill. "Hey, Bo, want to take a
ride with me?"

I gave a
woof and sat
down on Wyatt's
lap. He pushed forward
with his arms, and with
a *whoosh*, we were off! The
sled quickly gathered speed as
we headed down the hill. The wind
whistled past my ears. We were going
so fast! I barked nervously as Wyatt's
arms wrapped around me even tighter.
Right away, I felt so much better.

"My turn!" Imani called when we reached the bottom of the hill. "Want to come with me, Bo?"

I barked a no-thank-you—one sled ride was quite enough!

So as Imani and Wyatt headed back up the hill, I trotted off to find Comet.

"Hiya, Comet," I said as I found her outside the barn. "Are you enjoying the snow?"

"It's amazing!" she neighed. "I'm
so happy that I finally learned what
snow is!"

"I am too!" I said.

We decided to walk through the
meadow toward the woods.

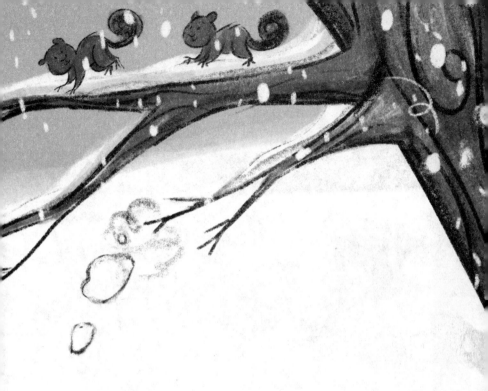

The forest was so quiet that we could hear the smallest sounds. I watched as a pile of snow fell off a tree branch with a soft plop. We could even hear the scampering of tiny squirrel feet crunching through the snow.

"Did you expect snow to be so fluffy and cold?" Comet asked.

"Nope, not at all, but I sure do love it!" I answered. "It's extra fun to roll around in."

When we returned to the barn after our walk, I heard something strange coming from the hayloft. It was a low groaning noise, and it didn't sound good at all.

Ice to See You

I needed to find out what was making that sound. What if one of the animals was hurt?

I climbed the steps up to the hayloft and noticed that the air was getting colder and colder the higher I went. The wind had picked up outside, and it was rattling the glass barn windows.

"Hello?" I called out. "Is anyone up here?"

There was no answer. So I waited a bit until I heard two low growls coming from the far end of the loft.

I looked up and saw four golden eyes glowing in the shadows.

It was the barn cats, King and Diva. My tummy squeezed tight. Bumping into them was never great news.

"Well, well, well, if it isn't Bo," King said as he stretched, flashing his claws and stepping slowly into the light. "What brings a little puppy like you into a place like this?"

"I heard a noise and got worried that someone was hurt," I said, standing my ground. I wasn't going to let the cats scare me off. "Is everything okay?"

Now Diva slunk over to us, stopping beside King. She let out a small cough and then hissed, "We are freezing our tails off in this ratty old barn. And now we are being bothered by a pesky puppy. Does that sound delightful to you?"

I thought about it. The freezing-cold part didn't sound delightful to me at all. I remembered how cold I was earlier, and I actually felt a little bit sorry for them. "No, it doesn't. But can I help?" I asked.

King sneered in a mean way.

"Ha! You? A *dog*? Help us *cats*?" he snapped.

"I was just trying to be nice," I whimpered with a shrug.

"Oh, Bo," said Diva. "Why don't you go dig a hole in the snow?"

"Or chase your tail and do some other silly dog things?" King added.

I knew King and Diva were trying to be mean, but these cats clearly had no idea how much fun digging holes and chasing your tail was. Too bad for them!

"Okay, but if you need anything, I'll be outside," I told them. The cats snickered as I started down the stairs.

They were not nice at all, but today I didn't mind too much.

"*Ice* to see you," Diva called after me. "But leave the loft to us cats."

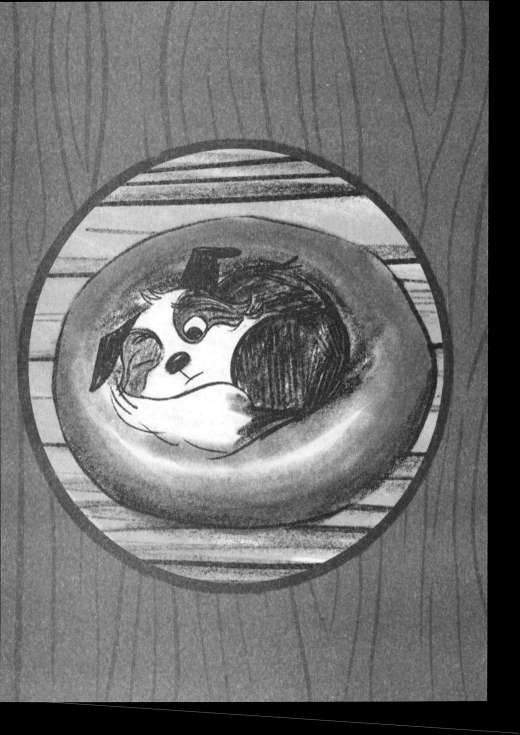

Blizzard Blues

That night I learned another fancy word: "blizzard." The snow fell faster and harder as evening came. The temperature dropped too.

I shivered as I curled up in the den. When my body started to warm up, I thought of the grumpy loft cats that I had seen earlier in the barn.

It was way too cold to sit inside by myself. I decided I had to help them!

But I needed a plan first. So I went over to Wyatt, who was sitting in front of the fireplace.

I grabbed the tip of his sock and pretended to play tug-of-war.

"Hey, what are you doing, Bo?" Wyatt asked. I gave a playful growl, shook my tail, and kept pulling.

When I finally got Wyatt's sock off, I jumped up and ran away with it. Imani, Wyatt, and our mom all chased me around the house, trying to get the sock back. They were shouting and calling for me to put the sock down.

Then Darnell came into the room
to see what was going on. He was
standing in the doorway, the door
propped open with his foot and his
arms full with a pile of chopped wood.

This was my chance! So I darted through the crack in the door and ran into the blizzard. If Wyatt wanted his sock back, he'd have to follow me outside to get it.

I dashed off the porch and landed in a fluffy, white snowdrift. It was hard making my way to the barn. The snow was so deep, I had to bounce my way there. The storm was getting worse.

Then finally I got to the barn and
waited for Wyatt and Imani to arrive.
When they reached me, I scooted inside
and hurried up the stairs to the hayloft.

King and Diva were still there
huddled together, shivering and
whimpering sadly. Thank goodness!
I'd gotten there just in time!

9

Safe at Home

Wyatt and Imani ran up the stairs after me, but they stopped when they saw me standing beside the barn cats. I whined, looked at the cats, and then turned back to the kids.

"Wyatt, look! Bo is trying to tell us that the cats are in trouble! Let's bring them back to the house!" Imani said.

They scooped up the cats and
nestled them beneath their winter
coats.

The cats meowed softly as we stepped outside. The snow was blowing even harder now. I led the way as we carefully headed back to the house.

When we reached the porch, Darnell and Jennica were standing by the front door waiting for us. "This is no time to be running outside!" Darnell cried.

"Dad, Bo saved the cats! King and Diva were freezing up in the hayloft, and Bo took us straight to them!" Wyatt explained.

"Oh, yes! I forget that the cats can't stay outside during a storm," Darnell replied with a sigh of relief. "The other animals prepare for the winter on their own naturally.

And things on the farm slowly change.
Horses grow thicker coats, pigs eat
more food, the sheep grow heavier
fleeces, and even the squirrels know
to gather and store extra acorns."

107

Darnell looked at me with a huge smile on his face. "But these poor cats just have each other . . . and of course you, Bo! You're such a good friend to remember to take care of our barn cats!"

"Can King and Diva stay here in the house, Dad? Please?" Imani asked. "It's so cold in the barn."

I let out a soft woof in agreement. "Well, if it's okay with Bo, then it's okay with me, too," Darnell said.

Life Is Good

Imani and Jennica wrapped the cats in blankets while Wyatt lovingly wrapped me up in a towel and rubbed me dry.

"You're such a good dog, Bo," he whispered as he scratched behind my ears. I loved it when he did that. It was the best feeling ever.

Then I went to my favorite blanket
by the fireplace and curled up. I was
surprised when King and Diva came
over to lay down beside me.

"Don't get too comfortable," King said. He looked at me with his golden eyes. "Dogs just don't smell nice enough to snuggle with every day."

"But once in a while, we can make an exception," Diva added lazily.

I knew it was hard for those cats
to say thank you. But I could see that
King and Diva were trying their best.

I closed my eyes and inched a little bit closer to them. And they let me.

Maybe tomorrow they would go back to being not so nice. But for tonight, life was good. We were all cozy and safe inside: my human family and I were together, the cats were warm, the chicks were cuddled in their nests, the pigs were in their pen, and the horses were snuggled in their stalls.

I opened my eyes and gazed out the window. The stars were sparkling in the cold night sky. It almost looked like the stars were winking back at me.

Then I put my head down and closed my eyes. This was the most perfect end to the most beautiful storm, and life couldn't get any better than this.

Here's a peek at Bo's next big adventure!

I love being a farm pup. There are so many animals to play with, and I'm lucky to have lots of friends! Take my good buddy Zonks, for example.

He's my pig pal, and his pigpen has the best mud on the farm. My favorite thing about him is that Zonks

An excerpt from *Barnyard Buddies*

is always down to play roll-in-the-mud. Pigs and mud go together like peanut butter and jelly.

I love playing in the squishy mud too, of course. But for some reason my humans are never very happy with me afterward. Whenever I come home after playing with Zonks, Darnell, my human dad, lets out a big sigh and rushes me to the bath every single time!

Then there's my friend Comet the foal. I can always count on Comet for a race around the farm. Horses are very strong, and they have really

An excerpt from *Barnyard Buddies*

long legs, so it's not easy to keep up with her, except if we're playing fetch. When it comes to fetch, I can run for miles. But if we're racing for fun, I usually just want to curl up for a nap after.

The baby chicks, ducks, and sheep, who are all so fluffy and kind, are my friends too. Seeing them always brightens my day. We play all sorts of games together, like hide-and-go-sheep and duck-duck-goose, out in the grassy meadow.

An excerpt from *Barnyard Buddies*